When This Box Is Full

By Patricia Lillie

Pictures by Donald Crews

PUFFIN BOOKS

PUFFIN BOOKS
Published by the Penguin Group
Penguin Books USA Inc., 375 Hudson Street,
New York, New York 10014, U.S.A.
Penguin Books Ltd, 27 Wrights Lane, London
W8 5TZ, England
Penguin Books Australia Ltd, Ringwood,
Victoria, Australia
Penguin Books Canada Ltd, 10 Alcorn Avenue,
Toronto, Ontario, Canada M4V 3B2
Penguin Books (N.Z.) Ltd, 182-190 Wairau Road,
Auckland 10, New Zealand

Penguin Books Ltd, Registered Offices:
Harmondsworth, Middlesex, England

*First published in the United States of America
in 1993 by Greenwillow Books, a division of
William Morrow & Company, Inc.
Published in Puffin Books, 1996*

10 9 8 7 6 5 4 3 2 1

LIBRARY OF CONGRESS CATALOGING-IN-PUBLICATION DATA

Lillie, Patricia.
When this box is full / By Patricia Lillie :
Pictures by Donald Crews.
        p.   cm.
Summary: Each month a child adds something
to an empty box, including a red foil heart in
February and toasted pumpkin seeds in
October.
ISBN 0-14-055831-4 (pbk.)
[1. Months—Fiction.] I. Crews, Donald, ill.
II. Title. PZ7.L632Wi 1997
[E]—dc20 96-34909 CIP AC

Printed in the United States of America

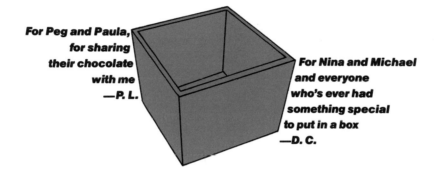

For Peg and Paula,
for sharing
their chocolate
with me
—P. L.

For Nina and Michael
and everyone
who's ever had
something special
to put in a box
—D. C.

This box is empty... but not for long.

I will fill it with...

January

a snowman's scarf,

January
February
March

**a red
foil heart,**

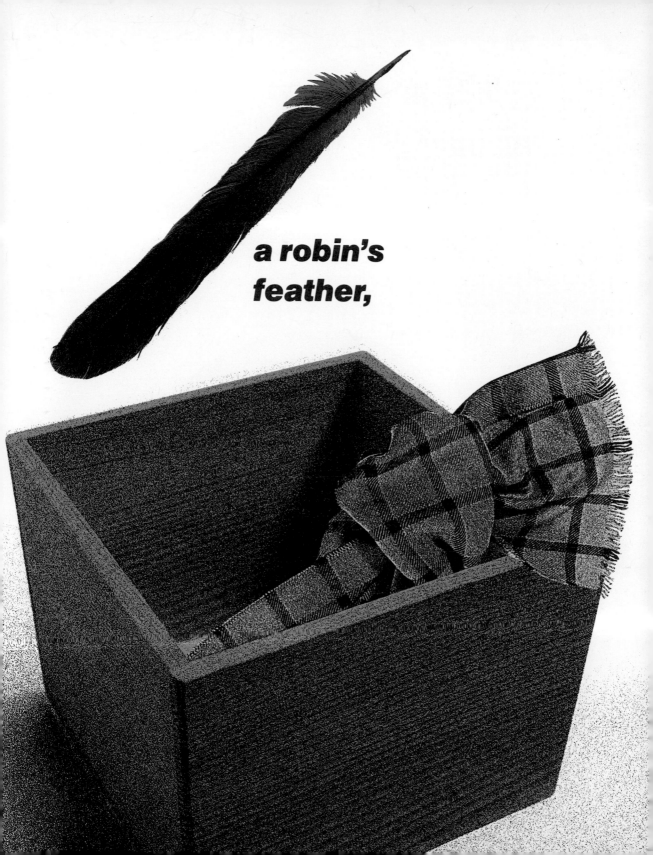

a robin's
feather,

**January
February
March
April**

**a purple
eggshell,**

January
February
March
April
May
June

a wild
daisy,

helicopters
from the
maple tree,

**January
February
March
April
May
June
July**

**a seashell
and some
sand,**

January

February

March

April

May

June

July

August

a ribbon
from
the fair,

January
February
March
April
May
June
July
August
September

**a red
leaf,**

January
February
March
April
May
June
July
August
September
October

toasted
pumpkin
seeds,

January
February
March
April
May
June
July
August
September
October
November
December

a wishbone,

and
a silver
star.

And then...

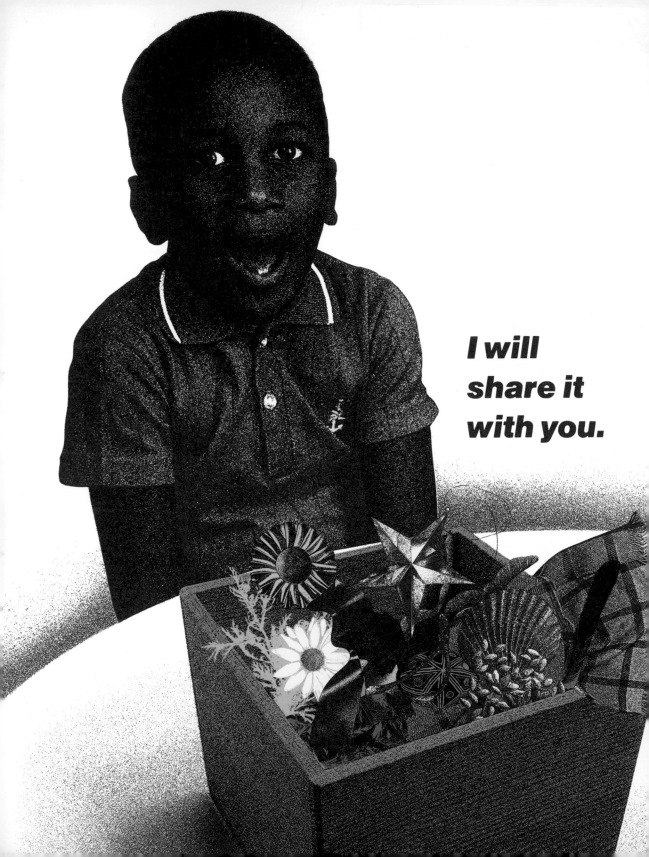

I will
share it
with you.